MRS PIG'S BULK BUY

Written and illustrated by
Mary Rayner

ATHENEUM NEW YORK

For Sarah, ketchup queen

Also by Mary Rayner

Mr and Mrs Pig's Evening Out
Garth Pig and the Icecream Lady
The Rain Cloud

and for older children

The Witch-Finder

Printed in Hong Kong

First American Edition 1981
Reprinted 1984

Library of Congress Cataloging in Publication Data

Rayner, Mary.
Mrs. Pig's bulk buy.

SUMMARY: The piglets are delighted when Mrs. Pig stocks up on ketchup, their favorite food, until they realize it's all they will be eating.
[1. Ketchup – Fiction. 2. Food habits – Fiction. 3. Pigs – Fiction] 1. Title.
PZ7.R2315Mk 1981 [E] 80-19875
ISBN 0-689-30831-0

A long time ago, when the piglets were very small, Mrs Pig went out to do the week's shopping as usual.

She left Sorrel and Bryony and Hilary and Sarah and Cindy and Toby and Alun and William and Benjamin and Garth at home with their father.

Mrs Pig went round the supermarket with a big shopping cart until she reached the tomato ketchup shelf. There she paused. An idea came to her, and a smile spread across her fat face. She put six enormous jars of ketchup into the cart, and went on with the rest of the shopping.

When she reached home all the little white piglets rushed down the hall to greet her.

"Hullo," they squealed. "What have you bought?"

And they began to pull things out of her basket, ripping open the bags of potato chips and packets of cookies and spilling them all over the floor. *Scrunch, scrunch* went their sharp little feet, and *munch, munch* went their greedy little jaws.

"Leave those things alone!" said Mrs Pig, cuffing them away with her hard trotters and picking up what was left of the potato chips.

She went into the kitchen and put the food away carefully in the cupboard. She placed the six jars of tomato ketchup on a high shelf and gave a little chuckle.

Usually, whatever she cooked for the children, they would be sure to ask for tomato ketchup on it. They had it on all the usual things such as egg and french fries, but that was not all.

They also spread it on their toast
in the mornings,

mixed it with their salad at dinner time,

poured it on their bread at tea

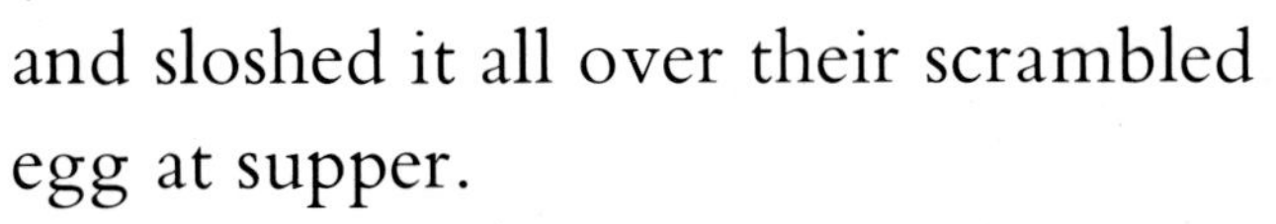

and sloshed it all over their scrambled
egg at supper.
Mrs Pig had been in despair.

No matter how carefully she flavored the stews or _____
spiced the puddings, the piglets always squealed for tomato ketchup. She had always tried to stop them from having it, and make one bottle last a week, but it was always gobbled up by Monday and then the piglets would grumble until she went to the supermarket again.

"But things will be different soon," thought Mother Pig happily. She reached down one of the big jars and emptied it into a huge soup tureen.

Then she set it on the table and laid the places for dinner. Father Pig had gone out. She called up to the piglets, "Dinner's ready!" There was a thunder of feet as the piglets ran downstairs and a shout of "Wait for me" from Garth.

"What are we having?" asked William Pig, and he leaned over the tureen and lifted the lid. "What's this?"

"That's your dinner," said Mrs Pig. "For the first time in your lives you can have as much tomato ketchup as you like. Help yourselves."

The piglets did not wait, but crowded round with their spoons, ladling out as much on to their plates as they could get.

"Isn't there anything else?" they asked.

"No," said Mrs Pig. "Not today."

The piglets were delighted. Never had they eaten so much tomato ketchup at one meal. Mrs Pig had to open the next jar when they all wanted second helpings.

The afternoon was fine and they all went out into the garden to play in the sand-pit. They made a long road for their cars and trucks.

William and Alun came in half way through the afternoon to ask for cookies, but Mrs Pig had shut the cupboard door and they could not open it.

By tea-time they were all hungry again. A large jam jar stood on the table, full of dark red liquid.

"Is it ketchup again?" they asked.

"Yes, as much as you want. And if you are very good, I might allow you half a piece of bread with it."

"Oh please, can we?" asked the pigs. So they were each given half a piece of bread.

After tea they watched television.

William and Alun went through to the kitchen again to see if there was anything they could find, but the food was safely out of reach in the cupboards, and Mrs Pig told them to wait until supper time.

When they arrived in the kitchen hoping for supper, the ten piglets were happy to see a pan on the stove bubbling away.

Imagine how upset they were when Mrs Pig poured out ten bowls of hot crimson liquid. "And that is all the supper you will have," she said.

"What, nothing else?" snuffled the piglets.

"If you are very good, you shall have half a cream cracker each with your ketchup."

And that is all they were allowed. It did not seem very much.

As they went up to bed they were feeling
uncomfortably empty.

The following morning Sorrel Pig bounced out of bed ahead of the others. School started again today.

She hurried downstairs. Cornflakes, she was thinking, and then a bowl of Rice Krispies, and perhaps some instant oatmeal if she could manage the kettle, and two slices of toast and butter and marmalade . . .

She opened the kitchen door and there, on the table, was the fifth jar of ketchup, surrounded by ten cereal bowls.

She tried the larder door. Locked. Sorrel did not feel like ketchup for breakfast, so she went off to school on the train without any breakfast at all.

When the other piglets came down and found nothing but the large jar they were not very happy either.

"Half a bowl of cereal with your ketchup, and that's it," said Mrs Pig, doling it out briskly. They were so hungry that they ate it, in spite of the way the ketchup lay in blobs and lumps stuck to their cornflakes.

Later that day Benjamin and Garth were given ketchup for lunch. The rest of them spent the day at school, but at dinner-time they opened their packed lunches to find no potato chips, no cookies, nothing but a ketchup sandwich each.

By that evening the piglets were desperate. "Please, Mum, don't get any more," they begged. "We just want food."

Mrs Pig beamed. "All right. I promise, no more big jars. Perhaps an ordinary little bottle now and then."

From that day on, the ten piglets had ketchup only on their egg and french fries. But the time when they had eaten it had done a strange thing. It had changed them all from being little white piglets into pink piglets, and all piglets have been like that ever since. The next time you see some, take a close look. You will see that under their white hair they are pink. So be careful with that ketchup bottle, or who knows, you just might turn really bright pink yourselves.

THE END